Coming Full Circle

By:Marva Loretta Young

Copyright © 2012

ISBN-13: 978-0-9848292-6-2

ISBN-10: 0984829261

Acknowledgments

I would like to thank my parents for their love and devotion over the years. You have been a support for me through everything. To my mom who will always give you the truth, even if it hurts.
I love you both.

To God be the Glory, I want to thank God for paving the way in my life and making this opportunity possible.

To all my readers: This is my first published novel and I hope you enjoy it. Please email me your feedback to marvayoung@gmail.com.

Prologue

As Reanna Leland tilted her head back against the airplane headrest, she thought over and over again why she chose to spend her vacation going to Atlanta for her college homecoming. The conversation she had with her college roommate and best friend, Kandra Lewis, two days ago replayed in her mind.

"When is your flight out for homecoming weekend, Wednesday or Thursday?" Kandra asked near the end of the conversation.

"Flight out for homecoming, I told you I was not coming, like I ever come!!!"

"Wednesday is" meet and greet" and Thursday the frat alumni are hosting the dance this year." Kandra stated as if Reanna never spoke.

"What don't you understand about, *like I ever come?*" Reanna nearly screamed into the phone.

"Come on it has been five years since we graduated and you still refuse to step foot on campus."

"You of all people should understand how I feel." Reanna exclaimed

"Look, I know Shawn hurt you more than you care to admit but that does not stop him from showing up every year like nothing ever happened." Kandra pointed out

"Spoken like someone that never had their heart broken by the person you loved more than life, not to mention, in front of all his frat brothers." Reanna's voice wavered on the last few words

"It was a graduation party, so Shawn was talking to his ex, which does not mean anything."

"In an upstairs bedroom?" Reanna said with tears in her voice. This was the only response she had because she never told anyone about the conversation she overheard that night.

"Reanna, just come and have fun, let him know that you are over him."

After much resistance from her and begging from Kandra, Reanna finally relented and agreed to come; she needed to get closure to this part of her life. Maybe Shawn could give her the information to help with that closure....

Chapter 1

After she finished her phone call with Kandra that night, she sat on her couch and thought about Shawn Remington, her first and only love, he always seemed to be in her thoughts lately. When she first met him they were both college freshmen, fresh out of high school. Shawn was there on a football scholarship and his moves on the field was nothing compared to the moves he made on her during their time together.

She met Shawn her first day at college during registration, he and a few of the freshman football team came in the main building and he ran right into her when she was on her way out the door. He grabbed her by the waist to steady her and that is when she looked up into the most intriguing caramel, brown eyes she had ever seen. His eyes were sparkling and his mouth had this cocky smile, and lord he had a dimple on the left side of his mouth. Reanna could just tip her head to the right side and put her tongue on his dimple and lick to her hearts content. He held her a little too close and long, as far as she was concerned, but who was complaining.

She saw him around campus occasionally after their initial meeting, and could not get the feeling of his touch out of her mind, but they did not start dating until the spring semester of their freshman year. She knew he was dating his high school sweetheart during the first semester of his freshman year; who attended the college across town, but she heard they broke up not long after the first month of school.

As she spotted him around campus that first semester she could not help but notice he was about 6' 2" and walked with the confidence of an athlete, or as they say he had a swagger about him. He definitely had the body of a wide receiver, broad shoulders and slim waist. He had cocoa brown skin and his cheekbones were high and distinct, almost like he was of an Indian heritage. He wore his hair in short, springy curls and always kept his edges trimmed.

Her first class of their freshman spring semester she bumped into him again; literally, going into her history class. He caught her by the arms this time and said "So we meet again."

"So I see, how are you, Shawn?' and she stressed the Shawn.

"I'm fine, you know my name?" he asked confused

"Yes, practically everyone on campus knows your name, football star and all. What are you doing here?"

Shawn blushed at the football star statement, "I am going to history class, what about you?"

"Ditto, it seems we have at least one class together this term." Turns out they had three classes together.

He asked her to be his study partner since they had so many classes together and their relationship blossomed from there. They seem to do everything together after they started dating, he walked her to class, took her to the movies, the mall, studied at the library together, and he also took her virginity that next fall the night before the football season opener. Reanna remembered it like it was yesterday, you only lose your virginity once....

. Reanna had her own hotel room because she wanted the privacy to finish They were out of town at the first football game of the season, their sophomore year, the football team traveled together and she carpooled with Kandra and a group of girls from their dorm a term paper for her history class.

It was a Friday, and she was supposed to meet Shawn for dinner at eight sharp in the lobby of the hotel. He was late getting to the lobby where they were suppose to meet, so she took a seat in the lounge to wait for him.

Shawn showed up fifteen minutes late and kissed her gently on the lips. "Sorry I'm late; practice lasted longer than I thought."

"No problem, I would wait for you forever if I had to."

Shawn touched her forehead, "you ok?'

"Naw, that term paper is kicking my butt, being sensitive must be one of the side affects."

"Don't front, you know you love me, come on let's grab a table." As the hostess directed them to the table, she noticed how many women turned and stared at the striking picture Shawn made and she felt lucky to have him.

Reanna ordered a chef salad and diet coke and Shawn ordered a steak and potatoes also with a diet coke. They talked about everything from school to their families during dinner; he also told her tales about his brother and sister during their childhood. Reanna enjoyed these tales because she was an only child.

Dinner went without a glitch until his cell phone rang. Shawn looked at the caller ID and rolled his eyes, "Let me answer this, baby."

"Shawn, can I help you?" he answered tersely. He listened intently and said,"I'm at dinner with ReRe, what's wrong." She knew there was a problem he seldom called her ReRe.

"Look, I will call your mom later and check on her. I am out of town at a football game. Yes, yes later tonight, bye." Then he disconnected the call and put the phone back in his pants pocket. He leaned back in his chair and rubbed his hands over his face in frustration, "I am sorry about that, baby."

"What was that all about?" Reanna questioned

Shawn stared at her a long time wondering if he should lie or tell her the truth, he chose the latter, "My ex-girlfriend from high school, her dad is in the hospital and is not doing well. She wants me to check on her mom later."

Reanna pursed her lips and said," The same one you were dating last year during your first semester in college? What's her name?"

Shawn looked up in surprise; he never knew Reanna knew about whom he was dating his first semester of college. "Her name is Melissa and yes the first semester girlfriend."

"Why is she still calling you, I thought you two broke up. I never knew you were still in contact with her." Reanna blurted out the questions in rapid succession.

Shawn took a deep breath and leaned forward placing both his forearms on the table, looking her dead in the eye, "Reanna, you have nothing to worry about. Melissa and I grew up together and she calls me occasionally to talk. I love you and when I asked you to be my girl that means I only want you, and only you. No one is ever going to come between us. "

Reanna's eyes misted at his declaration of love and she said, "I love you too." She leaned over and kissed him and as he shifted the kiss deepened and she felt the tingling all the way to her toes. They broke the kiss, Shawn paid for the meal and they went back to her hotel room to study.

Chapter 2

After a couple hours of studying, they decided to watch movies; she was still dressed in the red skirt set she wore to dinner, Shawn had on jeans and his football jersey.

They laid back on the bed and found the movie, *The Imitation of Life* on a local network station. Shawn was sitting halfway up, propped up against several pillows, leaning against the headboard, and Reanna had her head of Shawn's chest listening to his steady heart beat. As Shawn rubbed her back with his left hand and her thigh with his right, she felt a tingling in her lower abdomen region, what was wrong with her, she thought? Reanna began to shift to relieve the ache Shawn was creating.

Shawn shifted to look down at her, "Baby, what's wrong?"

Reanna's looked up at Shawn with glazed eyes full of desire and Shawn knew exactly what was wrong. "Shawn, I feel something and I don't know how to describe it, help me." Reanna heard the girls in the dorms discuss sex but she never realized the power it had over a person. She felt on fire, her nipples were tight and heavy and her vagina was already wet and overflowing. Shawn kissed her and Reanna flicked her tongue into Shawn's mouth over and over again. It seemed like they kissed forever before Shawn broke it off; he needed to catch his breath.

"Reanna, have you made love before?" Shawn asked her.

Reanna dropped her head and said "no" so softly he had to strain to hear her.

Hearing her answer, Shawn dropped his head back on the pillows and covered his eyes with his right forearm. Shawn was quiet for so long Reanna became worried, she touched the arm covering his eyes and he peeked from under his arm at her. "Shawn, what's wrong?"

"Reanna, you are a virgin and you don't understand what you are asking, I don't want to hurt you." "I love you and I know what I want, I want you." She leaned over and kissed him again and again. She might not know what she was asking for but she did know Shawn was the only man that can relieve her ache. As the kiss deepened, Shawn reached up and touched her left breast thru her blouse; he felt her shiver as he rubbed his hand over her nipple. He sat up from his reclining position and broke the kiss to nibble on her neck. She let out a low moan that made his already bulging manhood get harder. He took off her blouse and sat back to look at her breast encased in her beige lace bra. Her breast were nice and full and definitely in proportion with the rest her body he thought as he took a deep breath, trying to take it slow.

She unclasped her bra and her now full breast stood proud and erect, he leaned over to clamp a nipple between his lips. She groaned so loud and leaned back to give him better access.

He laid her down and pulled her skirt and underwear off. She lay before him with no clothes on and he took that moment to observe her body, full breast, tapered waist, full hips and long slender legs. God, what would he do if he ever lost her? He ran his hands over her breast, down to her hips and down her legs then up to her inner thighs. He took his time rubbing small circles in her inner thighs with his thumbs. Reanna was biting her lower lip and grasping the comforter with her hands. Shawn bent over and used his tongue to lick her inner thighs and belly button, he looked up at her and then put his tongue in her vagina, tasting her sweet juices. Reanna practically jumped off the bed at first contact, she felt so much love for Shawn at that moment she did not know what to do. Shawn flicked his tongue in and out of her until she screamed with frustration, then he latched on her nub and worked his tongue in slow circles around it until she was screaming for release. He then stuck a finger in her and sucking on her nub faster and faster until she cried out her climax. He took off his clothes and came up on the bed with her and kissed her gently, she looked at him through hooded eyes and said, "I love you." He kissed her again and put his hands between her thighs to feel how wet she was. He took her juices on his finger and wet her nub, she groaned again and he rose on his knees to put his condom on. He leaned over her and spread her thighs open. "Open wide for me, baby" he whispered in her ear. She did as he asked and he put his penis in the entrance of her vagina and pushed slowly into her. Reanna said," Please" and jerked her hips up. Shawn caught her hips and held them to the mattress he could not let her rush this; he did not want to hurt her. Shawn entered her again slowly inch by inch until he felt resistance, and then whispered "Baby, this might hurt." He pushed his way through the barrier and heard her cry out and stiffen up, he stayed still inside her as he licked her ear and rubbed her right nipple with his left hand. After a few moments, he felt her relax then started to move slowly in and out of her and Reanna was moving with him crying out his name. He came all the way to the end of her vagina and entered her fully again and again, they moved faster and faster until their orgasm came quick and hard.

They made love again, in the shower, before he left to go back to his hotel room. That night she knew she would love him forever.

Chapter 3

That same night after talking to Kandra about going to homecoming; Reanna made plane reservations for an early Wednesday flight to arrive in Atlanta, her thoughts went back to the night before graduation....

That day was the happiest in her life, Shawn had just proposed earlier that day and they were both going to work in Atlanta, she in a Finance consultant firm and he at an Accounting firm, they had it all worked out.

Earlier that day, they both agreed to meet at the graduation party at nine, which was taking place at Shawn's frat house. She had not heard from him since earlier that day, which was unlike him. He always made sure she had a safe way to any function that occurred on campus after dark.

Reanna arrived to the party with Kandra earlier than planned and it was in full swing, people were everywhere. The frat house was a two-story home located near the other sorority and fraternity houses on the campus.

Shawn moved into the frat house after he pledged during his sophomore year.

Reanna bumped into Tim and Randall, Shawn's line brothers, at the front door.

"Hey ReRe, what's shakin'?" Tim asked. Kandra cleared her throat waiting for an introduction, but Reanna ignored her, her first priority was finding Shawn.

"Where is Shawn?" Reanna asked with concern in her voice.

Reanna noticed Tim hesitated then said. "I saw him going to his room a few minutes ago, you know where it is."

Reanna turned to Kandra and said, "I will be back in a few minutes, I need to talk to Shawn."

Kandra kept scoping the crowd and gave Reanna a "later" as she walked away. As Reanna pushed her way through the crowd, she had the feeling that something was wrong, but she knew she had to get to Shawn so she could alleviate her fears.

She reached the stairs and took them one at a time; she knew Shawn's room was the last one on the right. As Reanna approached the room, the door was partially opened and she heard Shawn's voice and a woman's voice she did not recognize. She heard Shawn raised his voice and his statement made her breath catch in her throat and tears pool in her eyes.

"When were you going to inform me you were pregnant, I had to hear it from my mother?"

The woman was crying and gave a low, muffled response," I was going to tell you but every time I called you were too busy."

"Shit, Melissa I can't do this right now!!" Shawn exclaimed. Melissa his ex-girlfriend, Reanna thought as she leaned against the door. Reanna must have made a sound when she leaned against the door, because Shawn snatched the door open and all the blood drained from his face when he saw Reanna standing there.

By now Reanna had tears pooling down her face, her first and only thought was to turn and run; which is exactly what she did. She ran down the stairs, through the crowd, with Shawn behind her all the way calling her name. She made it outside, ahead of him, and ran all the way to her dorm room, stumbling in the dirt once, tears streaming down her face.

She cried all night and refused to answer his phone calls when he called her dorm and she cut her cell phone off completely. She packed the next morning, made it through graduation, and took the first flight back to Hilton Head to her parent's house.

She decided to take the second financial consultant job offer in Orlando, Florida; which is where she has called home for the past five years....

The voice of the flight attendant brought her out of her thoughts, "Please fasten your seat belts we will be landing in fifteen minutes." Kandra was meeting her at the Atlanta airport and they were going to the beauty parlor and nail salon before the "meet and greet" tonight.

As Reanna exited the plane and made her way to the baggage claim area, she pulled her iphone out of her purse to check her emails.

She heard a deep male voice from behind her say," You ready ReRe?"

She turned slowly and recognized Tim, Shawn's frat brother from college, standing before her with his hands clasped in front of him, "What are you doing here Tim?"

"Kandra was running late at work and coerced me into picking you up."

Reanna laughed at this, "Same old Kandra, I didn't know she still kept in touch with you. Wait until I get my hands on her."

Tim stared at her pensively for a moment, "There is a lot you don't know, maybe if you came around more."

Reanna rolled her eyes and said, "Stay in your lane Tim, stay in your lane." Reanna saw her luggage, out of the corner of her eye, rolling around on the turnstile and grabbed it. Tim took the luggage from her hands then turned and started walking toward the exit. They walked in silence until Tim approached a black hummer, and Reanna let out a long whistle of appreciation, "Wow Tim, you were always the big spender."

Tim peaked around at her from the rear of the car and stated matter of fact, "Don't hate, appreciate. Now get in the truck woman." Reanna hopped in and buckled up, ready for the ride.

Chapter 4

Reanna stared out the window as they drove along, a jazz cd playing, thinking of how she used to love Atlanta. Funny how life can throw a monkey wrench in your plans. She really didn't feel like talking but knew it was a matter of time before Tim broke the silence.

Sixty seconds later Tim took the plunge, so much for her moment of solitude. "What have you been doing with yourself these past few years?"

"Working in Florida, how about you?" Reanna tried to change the subject.

"Don't change the subject ReRe we are talking about you, not me. I always wondered why you disappeared so quickly after graduation."

"You are in the wrong lane again, Tim." Reanna quoted her earlier statement.

"Shawn had us tearing the campus apart looking for you after graduation, only to find out you were already MIA." Tim said with a sideways glance at her.

Reanna took a deep, shaky breath and said, "I have valid reasons for what I did back then, don't make me out to be the bad one here."

"I am not trying to place blame on anyone ReRe, I was curious why you left Shawn without even looking back. You two seemed so in love." Tim gave her a quick glance and took a sharp left turn.

"Where are you taking me?" Reanna questioned.

Tim rolled his eyes at her and chuckled, "I am taking you to your old Saturday morning hang out joint, at Kendra's request of course."

"Of course, and can you stop calling me ReRe it sounds like a name for a poodle." Reanna said as she licked her tongue out at him.

As Tim pulled up to the curb in front of the beauty/ nail shop, to drop her off, he laughed at her description of his pet name for her. He glanced past her through the windshields and smiled, "Here comes trouble."

Reanna turned in her seat to see Kandra running out of the beauty shop, arms wide.

Reanna jumped down from the Hummer and embraced Kandra in a big hug.

"I see you got here in one piece?" Kandra's said as she leaned around Reanna to look at Tim, who was exiting the driver's door. "Don't worry; you don't have to thank me." Tim said sarcastically as he approached the back of the Hummer to retrieve the luggage. As he transferred the luggage to Kandra's car Tim said, "You know you two really should be very grateful, it's not very often I agree to do favors, even if it is picking up old ReRe."

Reanna gritted her teeth and mumbled, 'I told you to stop calling me ReRe."

Kandra swatted her arm and laughed, "You know Tim was the only one brave enough to call you that."

"Brave enough or dumb enough, you choose." Reanna said as she laughed along with Kandra.

Tim glanced at his watch and decided to cut out while it was safe, "Sorry ladies I have to meet up with the guys in an hour, take care."

They waved him off and headed to get their beauty on. It took over three hours before they left the beauty parlor and arrived at Kendra's house in the Stone Mountain area of Atlanta, it was a two story house, painted burgundy and white. Kandra unlocked the door and Reanna entered the house she helped decorate. Since she knew the house like it was her own, Reanna headed upstairs to get prepared for the "meet and greet."

As she jumped out of the shower, she admired the beige and peach colors of the bedroom she decorated just for her short visits to see Kandra.   The colors always soothes her troubled mind, that seems to go haywire whenever she steps foot in Atlanta. She walked over to the walk-in closet and tried to choose the perfect attire for the "meet and greet" that was going to start without her if she did not get a move on. She took out a red clingy dress that would accentuate her full figure and black pumps. At five feet nine inches she had a perfect hourglass figure; most of her height was in her legs, which seem to be her greatest attribute. Her dark brown hair she kept at shoulder length, she had full, pronounced lips, high cheekbones, permanent arched eyebrows and her complexion was like marshmallow hot cocoa. She was at the mirror putting on her make-up when Kandra came in the room. She stopped when she got a glance at Reanna's attire, "Wow, you look great."

"I know, what do you think of the new pumps?" Reanna gave the perfect model's turn and struck a pose.

Kandra doubled over laughing, "You are crazy, you will be the envy of the party tonight."

"Not quite the affect I was looking for, I don't want to be the center of attention tonight." Reanna turned and looked at her reflection in the mirror.

"In that dress, guess again girlfriend. Now let's get a move on or we are going to miss the party." Kendra laughed again.

Chapter 5

Kandra pulled her white Camry into the parking space at the college cafeteria, where the "meet and greet" was being held. Reanna noticed the parking lot was full and the function had already started.

"Kandra, you could never be on time if your life depended on it." Reanna said as she leaned her head into her right hand.

"No, if I recall correctly you were always the one who made us late." Kandra said as she shifted to face Reanna.

"Maybe we can just go back to your house, change into our pajamas and watch movies?" Reanna suggested.

"Ummmm, let me see, no we will not give Shawn the satisfaction."

"This is not about Shawn, Kendra, I just want to try to enjoy this evening without any drama." Reanna pleaded.

"Drama is not in my vocabulary; now let's go make our grand entrance." Kandra unbuckled her seatbelt and hopped out the door.

Reanna stepped out the passenger side door a little slower than Kandra did and they met on the sidewalk in front of the car. Kandra looped her elbow thru Reanna's elbow and they walked toward the cafeteria together. Reanna knew her best friend was trying to make her feel comfortable with her decision to attend the homecoming functions but she still thought this was a bad idea.

As they crossed the threshold to the cafeteria Reanna's cell phone rang, she pulled it out of her purse and looked at the caller ID.

She turned to Kandra and said, "I need to answer this, I will catch up with you inside."

Kandra walked into the cafeteria as Reanna answered the phone, "Where are you at Reanna?"

"The meet and greet, where are you?" she questioned

"After finishing your work and mine today, I am heading to the airport to fly up to the ATL for homecoming, I will see there." Randall said.

Randall, Shawn's frat brother, took the position at the same Finance firm as Reanna when they graduated. Reanna begged Randall not to tell Shawn they worked together and so far for the past five years he has not disappointed her. They actually became best friends and she knew if Shawn ever found out Randall lied to him about their work/friendship there would be hell to pay in frat land. Randall's voice brought her thoughts back to the conversation, "I called to talk to you about something."

"What's up?" Reanna questioned cautiously

Randall hesitated then said, "Shawn called today and invited me to stay at his place for the homecoming weekend."

Reanna was quiet so long Randall thought they got disconnected, "You still there?"

"Yes, I am still here. Why would he all of a sudden ask you to stay with him? Do you think he found out we work together?" Reanna said all in one breathe.

"Don't concern yourself, I talk to Shawn occasionally and this is not so unusual, we are frat brothers." Randall reassured her.

"Ok, I guess you will have to call me this weekend because I would hate to call at the wrong time and have Shawn suspicious about who is on the other end of the phone."

"Look, I will call you when I get off the plane, after I get the rental car. Shawn and all the frats are getting together at his place tonight."

This was Randall's way of letting her know Shawn would not be at the "meet and greet."

"Ok, talk to you in a couple of hours then." Reanna said before she disconnected the phone and headed into the party.

She walked in and never saw Kandra again until it was time to go. She met so many of her old friends that she wondered, as they were leaving, why she stayed away so long.

Chapter 6

Her cell phone was ringing, pulling her away from her dream, a dream she did not want to wake up from. Shawn was just in the middle of telling her he loved her and as the phone rang again, she sat up abruptly waking from her dream. "Stupid phone, hello" she practically yelled into the phone.

Randall was talking in hushed tones; she could barely hear him, "Randall, why are you whispering?" Reanna whispered also.

"Look, just listen. I wanted to let you know I arrived safe and I can't talk long. All the line brothers are staying here at Shawn's house."

Reanna sighed, "Even Tim, you know Kandra had Tim pick me up from the airport."

Randall laughed, "So that's why Tim told the guys out loud that he saw you yesterday. I thought Shawn was going to snap him in half when he started bragging about how sexy your body was."

Reanna blushed even though no one could see her, "Tim did not do that!"

Randall laughed even harder, "Oh yes he did, I had to restrain Shawn from putting his hands around his throat. What happened between you and Shawn? I know he never got married and based on his reaction last night I think he still loves you. He was so protective of you back in college and he had the same reaction last night. I had to drag him out of the front room to calm him down."

"All you need to know is Shawn hurt me very bad and it took a long time to get over him and the pain." Reanna lay back in the bed and closed her eyes thinking of the pain she felt so long ago.

"Are you sure you are over him?" She suddenly heard a male voice in the background as Randall asked her the last question. She knew the voice belonged to Shawn, and her heart skipped a beat just knowing he was near.

Randall covered the mouthpiece and told Shawn "I will be there in a moment, let me finish this phone call." Shawn said something about people always working and never taking time off as his voice trailed off.

"Shawn is a trip; he has pictures of a little boy all over his apartment. I asked him about the photos and he said it was a long story." Reanna thought about the conversation she heard so long ago and wondered if this were the child he and Melissa were discussing five years ago.

"Look Randall I will see you tonight, call me later." Reanna cut off the conversation because she did not feel like lying to Randall if he asked her anymore questions about Shawn. She rolled over and fell asleep again resuming her dream about the man she knew she would always love.

After Reanna and Kandra woke up and got dressed, they hung out at the mall most of the afternoon shopping for new clothes to wear for the rest of the homecoming functions.

They ate lunch at a local Cajun cuisine restaurant and then headed home to rest before the dance. They woke up from their nap late and had to rush to make it to the dance on time. The dance was being held at one of the ritziest hotels in town; Reanna thought, leave it up to the frat brothers to do it up big.

As they arrived at the dance and walked through the double doors Kandra poked her in the side and pointed to the corner where Shawn and his frat brothers were hanging out.

Reanna decided to head in the opposite direction and took a seat at a corner table.

"Reanna, you can't hide forever." Kandra sat down beside her with a sigh.

"I am just collecting myself, give me a minute." As a waiter passed by Reanna grabbed a glass of white wine off the tray. She took a long sip of the wine and sputtered.

"Take it easy girl." Kandra said as she patted her on the back. They sat in silence for a few more minutes then Kandra decided to make her way around the room leaving Reanna sitting at the same table still trying to regroup.

Reanna grabbed another glass of wine from a passing tray and sipped it in less time it took her to finish the first glass. She felt a migraine coming on; she could never drink more than one glass of any brand of alcohol without getting a headache.

She rubbed her temples as her migraine increased and knew she needed to go lay down somewhere. She did not see Kandra anywhere but spotted Randall through the crowd still huddled up with his frat brothers. Reanna got up, on shaky legs, and made her way slowly over to Randall. Her head was hurting so bad she gave little thought to the fact that Shawn was also in the group. She approached Randall and touched his forearm before saying,"Randall, could you please take me home?'

Randall turned to her slowly with an inquisitive look on his face as all the frat brothers in earshot, including Shawn, stopped and took notice of her question.

Randall could look in her eyes and tell something was wrong, "You ok, Reanna?"

Knowing something had to be wrong for her to approach him in front of everyone.

She rubbed her temples and shook her head slowly, "My head hurts. Can you drive me home?" She said so low it came out in a soft whisper. Shawn stepped around the other brothers and turned her slowly to face him, she looked up at him and sighed, "My head hurts Shawn, and I want to lie down."

Shawn asked her in a soft, low tone, "How many drinks have you had Reanna?"

"Two" but she raised three fingers. Shawn cursed as he scooped her up in his arms and headed towards the door, Randall started to follow them but the look in Shawn's eyes stopped him dead in his tracks. "I will deal with you later." Shawn said to Randall on his way out as he brushed past all the frat brothers.

He went to the elevators and when the door opened he entered it and pushed the floor number to take her to the hotel room he rented for the night. Leaning against the wall of the elevator he looked down into her face, as he held her tighter in his arms, and wondered what went wrong between them. He knew if she knew the details of what really happened the night before graduation she would never forgive him for the choices he made. He opened the door to his room and walked over to the bed and gently laid her on the covers, "Reanna, do you have your migraine pills on you?"

Her eyes fluttered open slowly and she raised her right hand to touch his face, "In my purse, where is Randall?" Shawn ignored her question about Randall because he would deal with him later.

He reached for her purse and retrieved two migraine pills and went to the refrigerator and took out a bottle of water for her to take the pills. After she swallowed the pills, he undressed her down to her slip, tucked her under the covers and gave her a kiss on the forehead. He stood there looking at her sleep, for what seemed like an eternity, before heading to the door to find out what the hell was going on between her and Randall.

Chapter 7

Shawn strode from the elevator with a determined stride; his only thought was to find out why Reanna went to Randall for help, because as far as he knew she wasn't ever that close to any of his frat brothers. He entered the dance and scanned the crowd for Randall, when he couldn't locate him he walked over to the group of frat brothers to inquire about Randall's whereabouts. They all looked uneasy and hesitated to give him any information.

Shawn sighed and looked them all in the eye, "Look you guys, I need to talk to Randall, if I have to find him myself the more pissed off I am going to get. So either you tell me where I can find him or I tear this place apart until I do."

Tim stepped up to face Shawn, "Please just listen to him first before you react, he went out the door to the pool area. Take it easy on him."

Shawn brushed past Tim and headed towards the door leading to the pool area. When he stepped out the door he saw Randall sitting in a pool chair, leaning forward, with his elbows on his knees glaring into the water. Shawn approached him and took the seat next to him; they sat in silence just glaring into the pool until Randall leaned back in his chair and looked at Shawn.

Shawn leaned forward and looked Randall dead in the eyes, "You have something to tell me, and don't you dare lie to me."

Randall knew by his tone that it was not the time to question Shawn about anything, but Reanna was his best friend and he had to make sure she was ok.

"Where is Reanna?" Randall asked as he tried to prepare himself for the explosion he knew was coming soon.

"In my hotel room upstairs sleeping off her migraine, she never could handle alcohol without getting headaches. Let's quit beating around the bush, I want you to tell me why Reanna felt the need to come to you for help. When did you get to be so close to her and make sure you think about what you say because I would hate to have to whip your ass." Shawn stated in a matter of fact tone.

Randall stood up and walked to the edge of the pool, then turned around, with his hands on his hips, took a deep breath and plunged in, "Reanna and I have worked together at the same finance firm for the past five years, since we left college. She and I really got to know each other and we are very close friends. She asked me not to tell you and that was a decision I made, so don't blame her."

Shawn was quiet so long that Randall finally decided to break the silence, "I am sorry frat but she really needed a friend after you two broke up, she never told me what happened between you two and I never asked. I want you to know nothing ever happened between us and we have a very close, platonic relationship."

At that last statement, Shawn decided to comment, "I hope for your sake it was only platonic, I can't believe all those years I talked to you, you never said a word. You really are a piece of work!"

"It was not like that Shawn, she needed a friend!" Randall practically yelled.

Shawn jumped out of his seat, knocking the chair he was sitting in over," Bullshit, every single one of you knew I was searching for her and you, you really crossed the line, and we have a brotherhood oath that you obviously care nothing about."

Shawn clenched and unclenched his fist at his sides wanting to punch something. He decided instead to turn and walk away before he did something he would regret. On his way to the door he turned back around and said, "As far as I am concerned we are no longer frat brothers."

Shawn walked back thru the crowded party, speaking to people as he passed them on his way back to his room to check on Reanna. He made it to the room in record time, when he walked in the bedroom Reanna had kicked off the covers and her slip had worked its way up past her hips. Shawn looked at her lace panties and reached his hand down to touch her thigh, it was soft as silk just like he remembered. He always loved her long legs especially when they were wrapped around his hips during one of their lovemaking sessions. He felt his manhood coming to life just thinking about how it used to be. He took one last look before covering her up again and went in the lounge area to watch some television and maybe get some work done on his laptop.

Reanna woke up disoriented and lifted her head slowly; she did not know where she was or how she got there. The last thing she remembered she had a headache, which was almost gone. She got out of bed and went to use the restroom, looking in the mirror she ran her hands through her hair and wondered how she got out of her clothes. Walking back in the bedroom she looked at the clock and it read three am, she crossed the room to the lounge area and stopped when she Shawn sleeping on the rollout bed. Seeing Shawn, it all came back to her and she sat in the arm chair and groaned, she must have groaned too loud because Shawn sat up in the bed and looked at her. They stared at each other, then suddenly Shawn held a hand out to her and she got up in what felt like slow motion and went to him. Shawn said, "Hey beautiful, how you feeling?" as she sat on the edge of the bed.

Reanna held her head down shyly and mumbled," I feel better, thanks." She looked up into his eyes and felt like she was drowning all over again. He leaned over and palmed her face with his hands, "You are so beautiful." He said right before he kissed her. He nibbled on her lips and brought his hand down to her shoulders dragging her on top of his body as he leaned back on the pillows. He ran his hands from her shoulders, across her back and down to her hips to palm her buttocks.

Reanna could feel her body on fire especially in her lower region of her pelvic area; he always affected her this way. She parted her legs to straddle him to give him better access to her vagina, he ground against her and she groaned her pleasure. He kissed and nibbled on her lips until they felt swollen and bruised.

She removed her slip and bra and he exclaimed in a passion filled voice, "I missed you, ReRe. You are so beautiful." He brushed his thumbs across her nipples and her eyelids fluttered closed as he leaned up to bring one nipple in his mouth. She arched her back and moved her vagina over his penis in a circular motion. She stood up over him and removed her panties, knowing he was already naked underneath the covers, she remembered he always slept in the nude.

She peeled back the covers and was not disappointed because he was as naked as the day he was born. He was so hard and she reached down to touch him, his whole body jerk on first contact. He groaned as she rubbed him from the tip to the sac area, over and over again. She loved how powerful he always made her feel. Shawn had enough of the torture and flipped her over beneath him; he kissed her again as he put his fingers between her thighs and rubbed her nub. She arched off the bed and cried out his name as he worked her nub in a circular motion and then stuck a finger in her moist crevice. She did not think she could take anymore and cried out, "Please Shawn, I need you now."

Shawn looked down at her and reached over to get a condom from his pants and rolled it over his erection. He brought his penis to her entrance and pushed into her slowly, feeling resistance he hesitated. She kissed him and rubbed her thumbs along his cheekbones, "It has always been only you." He pushed all the way in her and moved slowly in an out of her, increasing his pace as he went. They moved in perfect accord and when their orgasm came they cried out each others names.

Chapter 8

Reanna woke to the most wonderful feeling; someone was nibbling her ear and running their hand along her thigh. She moaned and scooted back into the body heat she felt behind her. She knew this was not normal and her eyes snapped open. She rolled over and was looking into those captivating, caramel eyes she had been seeing in her dreams the past five years. "Morning, sleepyhead," Shawn sat up and propped several pillows behind his head. Reanna sat up slowly and leaned back on the headboard with her eyes closed. "Shawn, what are we doing? We can't turn back the hands of time." Reanna shifted around to face him pulling the sheet up over her breast.

Shawn stared at her for a few seconds then she heard her cell phone ring from the next room, "That would probably be your boy Randall checking up on you." Shawn sarcastically stated.

"There is nothing going on between Randall and I, he is just a friend." Reanna said defensively.

"And co-worked I gathered from the conversation I had with him last night." Shawn threw his legs over the side of the bed after throwing out that little tidbit of information. He walked into the other room and returned with a towel around his waist and her cell phone in his hand. He handed her the cell and kissed her, "Call Randall and let him know you are fine because if he calls again I won't be responsible for my actions next time I see him. I am going to take a shower."

When she heard the shower running she made a quick call to Randall and Kandra to let them know she was ok, then she got up and walked straight to the restroom. How dare Shawn confront her friends and try to run her life, he was the one who hurt her. She snatched up a towel and wrapped it around herself and opened the shower stall and stepped in, ready to do battle. Shawn turned slowly towards her and leaned against the shower wall, looking her up and down, "You are a little overdressed for a shower woman."

"Don't do this to me Shawn, I know we made love last night but it means nothing. I have a good life and I can't do this with you again." He pushed off the wall and came to stand in front of her placing his palms on the shower wall above her head and leaned down to kiss her. He kissed her again and again until he felt her relax, her hands now resting on his hips. He released her towel and it dropped to the shower floor, lifting her up until she clasped her legs around his waist. "I miss you, Reanna. There has never been anyone but you in my heart since you left." He entered her swiftly, her back against the wall now. He started a little rocking motion, in and out, "You feel so good, baby." He groaned out against her throat. Reanna couldn't take much more as she cried out and shivered as an orgasm came upon her. A few minutes later Shawn pushed deep into her as his release came. He released her and her legs dropped to the shower floor, his hands still on her hips to steady her. Shawn grabbed her chin and let her know, "I want you in my life again, and I know there are some things that you need to know. Things are not what they seem and I need you to understand that I love you and I have always loved you. I will talk to you Sunday after church at my mom's house; we will have privacy and time to talk then." Reanna nodded and reluctantly agreed, not knowing if things would ever be ok again.

The rest of the weekend went by in a blur, Reanna spent Saturday with Shawn, they arrived at the picnic together, went to dinner together and that night he took her back to Kandra's house. They planned to meet at the church the next morning which was the final activity of the homecoming weekend.

Reanna and Kendra arrived at the church early and attended Sunday school; they were out front waiting for church to start when Shawn pulled up in his black BMW.

Reanna already spoke to Shawn's mom and siblings, and could not wait to see him again. She knew his father died a few years ago, but Shawn never talked about him much, not even during their college days.

They spoke briefly last night before she went to bed and she missed him already. He came bounding up the steps in a blue double breasted suit, looking like he came straight out of GQ magazine. He leaned over and kissed her as he stood next to her. "Good morning baby." Reanna blushed and Shawn thought she never looked more beautiful in her burgundy suit and beige pumps. He reached over and grabbed her hand with his and turned to head in the church when they heard a young child holler, "Dad wait for me, wait for me!"

Reanna felt Shawn's tense next to her and turned to catch the child in his arms. "Dad, we surprised you!" Shawn turned to Reanna and looked in her eyes and mouthed "trust me, please." Reanna felt like her breath was being cut off, felt tears pool in her eyes and turned away for a few seconds to get composed.

When she thought it couldn't get worse, the woman's voice from so long ago came through clear as day, "Shawn, Sam wanted to surprise you today."

Reanna and Shawn both turned to see Melissa standing there, "What are you doing here, Melissa?" Shawn narrowed his eyes at her as he spoke.

Shawn's brother, Stan, saw the storm brewing from across the church grounds and came and lifted Sam out of Shawn's arms, "Sam lets see what your grandma and auntie are up to." He headed in the church doors, Sam in tow, leaving the three of them standing on the steps

. "Sam and I came to be with the family today. I heard you were back with your old girlfriend, what happened she forgave you?"

Shawn stepped toward Melissa, "Don't mess with me Melissa, you definitely don't want to cross me."

Melissa didn't take the warning and pressed on. "Did you tell her about our son?" Reanna gasped and moved to get around Shawn but he stopped her by grabbing her around the waist. "Please Reanna, don't." Shawn begged not wanting to lose her again. He pressed her head in his shoulder and held her close.

"Let her go she walked out before, without giving you a second thought." Melissa kept pushing.

"Shut up, Melissa!" Shawn hissed about to lose his control.

Reanna squeezed his arm to remind him where they were, "Shawn, please don't do this here." She pleaded with tears in her eyes. Shawn grabbed her hand and they turned and walk into the church, sitting in a pew behind his family. The service was great and when alter call came Reanna stayed kneeling there so long that Shawn had to go get her and bring her back to the pew. She did not see Melissa during the service but Sam came to sit with them, holding Shawn's hand and glancing up at Reanna every now and then.

Chapter 9

After church they drove to Shawn's family house in silence; Reanna staring at the passing scenery wondering what she had stepped back into. Shawn broke the silence, "I am sorry about what happened at the church, just please give me a chance to explain everything."

"You don't even seem like you like her, how can you two raise a child together?" Reanna questioned.

Shawn took a deep breath, "He's not mine." Reanna jerked her head up and stared at him. "I will explain everything later, he is family and yes he calls me dad, but he is not my child." Reanna's head was spinning wondering what in the world Shawn was talking about, she finally decided to wait until later and get the details.

By the time they arrived at the house everyone was already seated for Sunday dinner, Shawn held out her seat for her and then sat down next to her.

"Dad, you made it?" Sam exclaimed. Reanna did not see Sam when she walked in but he was seated next to Shawn's mom at the other end of the table. Shawn leaned forward and blinked at him, "Yes sport, I made it."

When Shawn saw everyone was finished eating dinner he stood and informed everyone, "Reanna and I will be in the back office." His mom waved them off and said, "You two love birds have fun." Shawn led her to the back of the house and stood back so she could enter the office ahead of him. He locked the door behind them and took a seat on the leather couch, leaning his head back on the cushion.

Reanna walked over to the couch and slid into his lap, placing her head on his chest. Shawn held her for several seconds before he started talking, "You were my heart back in college and I would've done anything to have things turn out different. I almost lost it after you left; I was on a downward spiral and if my brother didn't come to my rescue..." He left that sentence hanging.

"Melissa came to me that night before graduation to tell me she was pregnant, but not by me, she was having an affair with my father." Reanna looked up him, her mouth wide open. "She was having an affair with my father, got pregnant and when my mother found out she was pregnant, she thought it was mine. The sad part is that the night I came to this house to confront my father he had a stroke and died. My sister, brother and I felt my mother was in enough emotional pain so the easiest thing was to let her keep thinking Sam was mine." Reanna knew she could never give Shawn children because of cist on her ovaries, she has had several operations over the years to remove them. Each operation left her fallopian tubes scarred.

"You have been supporting him this whole time?" Reanna asked.

Shawn shook his head, "No, Melissa is being paid out of a trust fund we set up for him from my dads insurance money. That is why I was surprised to see her today; this was not Sam's weekend to be with us. I never have deal with her personally; it is usually Stan or a family member that contacts her about things concerning Sam."

Reanna leaned up and kissed him on the lips, loving him more for the man he became. "I have an early flight out tomorrow and I am going straight to work when I get back." Reanna slipped in.

Shawn rubbed her hip with his fingers and nibbled her jaw line, "Come home with me tonight. I will drive you to the airport tomorrow morning." As he nibbled down her neck she tried to speak, "My things…are at Kandra's, and I will need to pick my things up before we go to your place."

They left his moms house and picked up her things from Kandra's, and headed across town to Shawn's townhouse. He lived in a townhouse in the Stone Mountain area and when they arrived he took her on a tour and then went back out to the car to retrieve her bags. She was sitting on the couch when he got back watching TV, he put her bags in an upstairs bedroom and came back to sit next to her. She was still in her burgundy suit but had long since abandoned her shoes and stockings and as she sat there her skirt had slipped up to her lower thigh level. Shawn reached over and pulled her onto his lap so she straddled him, her skirt coming all the way up to her waist.

He was running his hands up and down her thighs, holding her eyes captive with each stroke. "Marry me, Reanna. I want you here with me." Shawn kissed her and waited for her reply.

"I think we should take it slow and see where this takes us, Shawn; I don't want us to end up hurting each other again." She leaned up and kissed him bringing her body flush with his. She unbuttoned his shirt and parted it, leaning down to lick his nipples then suck on them. Shawn groaned and threw his head back. She climbed off his lap and unbuckled his belt, pulling his pants and boxers off. He was naked except for his socks; she kneeled in front of him and touched his penis. She brought the head of his penis to her lips and licked on it over and over with her tongue, while he jerked his pelvis forward. She opened her mouth and took his entire penis in and sucked on him, making puckering sounds with her jaws. When Shawn could take no more he pulled her up, discarded her clothes, slid on a condom and pulled her up to straddle him. She positioned him outside her entrance and slowly lowered herself down on him. He kissed her breast and tweaked her nipples with his forefinger and thumbs, raising her level of excitement with each touch. She leaned back putting her hands on his thighs for support and moved up and down, faster and faster. She could feel her orgasm building and rode him faster, and then she saw flashing lights explode behind her eyes and felt him tense beneath her. She had her second orgasm as she felt his penis contract against the walls her uterus. They made love again later that night this time with her on her stomach, him entering her from behind. He made

this time nice and slow; he wanted her to remember who she

belonged to.

Chapter 10

After a long flight home, Reanna went back to work and jumped right in. She knew her trip would put her behind but she felt she would never put a dent in the paperwork on her desk.

She had been back three days and still more paperwork, time for one of her and Randall's working dinners. She picked up the phone and dialed Randall's extension,

He picked up on the second ring. "Randall, may I help you?"

"You made it back I see, how are you?" Reanna tapped her finger on the desk as she looked out the window.

"Fine, I thought you forgot about a brother." Randall threw in.

Reanna threw her head back and laughed. "No, I have just been busy catching up on work. Listen, how about we do one of our working dinners, I need to get caught up and I am sure you could use some help."

Randall was silent for a moment, "Sure, Friday at six, your house or mine?"

Reanna thought a moment, "My house is fine, and I will cook. See you then."

Friday night Reanna was in the kitchen finishing up the meal and Randall was setting up the work area when her telephone rang. "Grab that for me Randall my hands are full." Reanna shouted as she took the roast out of the oven.

She heard Randall carrying on a conversation with someone and wondered who it could be, moments later he pushed through the kitchen door and handed her the phone. "Shawn wants to talk to you." He walked out of the room and licked his tongue out at her. "Hey Shawn, how are you?" Her voice came out sounding a lot more casual than she felt.

"A working dinner, what is a working dinner?" Shawn's voice lowered an octave.

"I am sure you did not call to lecture me about Randall, and a working dinner means we are both behind on our work and now we are going to pull an all night session, if necessary, to get caught up." She explained as she put plates and silverware on the counter. "I called to tell you I love you and I will be there on business in two or three weeks, depends on my schedule."

Reanna leaned against the counter and closed her eyes. "I miss you and can't wait to see you." Reanna and Shawn caught up on the week and then Reanna and Randall spent the night getting caught up on their paperwork

Shawn came to town two weeks later on business. Reanna didn't see much of him but they did visit one of the theme parks when he was in town. The trip was a short one and Shawn took the first flight out Sunday morning back to Atlanta

Reanna didn't know what was wrong with her, she felt tired all the time and her stomach would not settle down. She called out from work the last few days and did not think she could make it this morning either. Maybe she got the flu from Randall last week, she was working with him and the whole office was spreading it around. She made herself get up and go to her doctor's appointment, she needed to get well and get back to work.

An hour later she walked out of her doctor's appointment in a daze, she needed to call Shawn. How was she going to tell him after all he had been through. While she was standing on the sidewalk thinking about her options her cell phone rang. She picked it up without checking the caller ID. "Hello."

"Reanna, you ok?" Her mom asked her. "You called last night and when we travel we never get the messages right away." Her parents never stayed home since they retired three years ago. "I am fine mom, I was feeling under the weather the past few days but I am fine now." Reanna could not tell her mother she got pregnant by her college sweetheart during the first homecoming weekend she has attended since graduation. She also did not know how she was going to tell Shawn, the doctors told her she could never have children. Now she was six weeks pregnant.......

Chapter 11

It was the night of the annual company fundraising party, attendance was mandatory for all staff members. She was four months pregnant and still has not told Shawn about his impending fatherhood. She knew her time was up; this was the function that all the frat brothers supported and attended. Shawn called her early to tell her he just got into town and he would see her there. She dressed in a light blue dress that flowed freely around her body and fell just below her knees. She had to buy new pumps with low heels; she wore her pearl necklace and earrings to finish off the outfit.

Randall had the limo pick her up at seven thirty pm; she arrived at the company offices by eight pm. Randall met her at the limo concern in his eyes. " Melissa showed up and Shawn is not too happy about it."

"What is Melissa doing here?" Reanna put her hands on her back feeling a little discomfort.

Randall shrugged his shoulders and escorted her in the banquet room. Reanna looked around for Shawn and saw him in the corner arguing with Melissa. When he saw her he put his glass on the nearest table and hurried over to her, slowing down his pace as he got closer to her.

"You look good Reanna, more radiant." Shawn noticed looking her up and down.

Reanna stepped up to him and gave him a kiss on the lips, "I really need to talk to you before the night is over." She felt another twinge in her back and put one hand up to rub the spot and the other hand on her stomach to help alleviate the pain.

She knew Shawn was saying something to her but it seemed so far away, she was falling into a black hole. Shawn caught her as she passed out.

She woke up hours later in a hospital room, hooked up to tubes and blinking machines. She turned her head and saw Shawn leaning back in the chair, next to her bed, eyes closed. Although he was breathing evenly, she knew he was not asleep. As her nurse breezed in to take her vitals, Shawn slowly got up out of the chair and went to glare out the window, hands shoved deep in his pants pockets. He waited for the nurse to leave before he spoke. "When were you going to tell me you were pregnant?" She knew he was angry but he would not stress her right now.

Reanna's eyes filled with tears. "I wanted to tell you in person but you never came back into town after the first visit. I was going to tell you tonight that is why I told you I wanted to speak to you."
"I knew we didn't use protection when we made love in the shower but I assumed you were on the pill." Shawn faced the window again as he made this statement.

"Shawn, the doctors told me I probably would never get pregnant, I have had complications before. I am sorry, what are the doctors saying."

Shawn turned to face her again. "You will have to go on bed rest for the rest of your pregnancy, you were spotting. I have made plans for us to get married here tomorrow." Her eyes got wide at his last statement.

"I will be in town until you are released and I am taking you back to Atlanta, if you can travel. If you can't travel I will transfer to the Orlando office and work from there." He walked over to her and kissed her lightly on the lips. "You scared me to death when you passed out. Wow, we are going to having a baby."

Chapter 12

They got married in the hospital, the next day, with only close friends and family around; they decided to have a reception after the baby was born. Reanna was in the hospital for two weeks and the doctor gave her the ok to travel when she was released. They didn't travel back to Atlanta until a week after she got out the hospital; they decided to move into his mom's house until after the baby was born, that way his mom could stay with Reanna in the daytime.

Reanna's days were spent sleeping, reading and watching television. The months were running into each other, she rarely saw Shawn and this made her lonely. He seems to be always working or too tired to talk when he came home. He took business trips out of town one weekend a month. They had minor disagreements and seldom talked lately.

Reanna knew one time when they disagreed, Shawn left and never came back until the next morning. Their marriage did not seem like a marriage at all. He never really touched her or held her lately, even though the doctors said they could resume their "marital relations."

She was in her sixth month of pregnancy when Shawn came home earlier than usual from work. Reanna looked up as he walked in the room. "Hi, you're home early are you ok?" She placed the magazine she was reading on the bed.

Shawn was taking his tie off as he walked into the room." Yes, just have to get ready for the father/son banquet the firm is having tonight." He walked over and kissed Reanna on the lips.

"Oh, when do we leave for the banquet? I can be ready in an hour. What time is it?" Reanna swung her legs over the side of the bed sitting up awkwardly because of her pregnancy.

Shawn shook his head. "Reanna you need to take it easy and the doctor said bed rest." He sat on the bed beside her, holding her hand.

Reanna shook her head. "Shawn, I am pregnant not disabled, please I am going crazy staying in this house all day. The doctor said I can go out occasionally as long as I don't overdue it." Shawn took a deep breath and looked at her. "No, I can't risk something happening to you and the baby. I have to be there in two hours and Stan will be here to pick up mom a little after that to take her. Melissa will probably bring Sam and that is stress I don't want you to deal with."

"You know me better than that I can handle Melissa; her words mean nothing to me." Reanna stood up and looked at Shawn. "I really would love to spend time with you; we haven't spent that much time together since we moved back here."

Shawn stood up and started to disrobe and getting items together to take a shower. He walked into the bathroom and came back out with a towel wrapped around his waist.

"So you are going to ignore me?" Reanna held her arms across her protruding stomach and rolled her eyes. "I just told you I want to spend time with you and you ignore me."

Shawn stopped, with his hand on his hips, as he was headed back into the restroom and turned to face her. "I don't want to argue with you about this and yes I would love to spend time with you. I should be back by ten or eleven. I don't want you going out." He then turned and entered the bathroom to shave and take a shower.

Reanna sat on the bed and could not believe the way her marriage was going. Shawn finished his shower, dressed up in dress pants and shirt, kissed her and left. Reanna was not finished with this yet; she had a surprise for him.

Shawn was sitting at a table with Tim, Sam and several co-workers discussing the current happenings in the news when Tim leaned over and pointed towards the entrance doors. "Here comes your mom, you didn't tell me Stan was bringing ReRe with him."

Shawn turned around in his seat to see Reanna, in a red ruffled maternity dress, on his brother's arm and they were heading towards a table across the room. "I assumed she was staying home since she was on bed rest."

Tim gave a low whistle. "Wow, she is sexy even pregnant. You are a lucky man." Tim laughed when Shawn cut his eyes at him. "Don't take it personal man, you married a sexy woman."

Shawn stood up and leaned over towards Sam and said, "Little man, I am going to see Reanna, I will be right back."

Sam jumped out of his chair and turned around looking for Reanna, "ReRe is here, I see her, I will be right back."

Shawn gave a puzzled look at Sam and followed him over to where Reanna was seated with his family. He kissed his mom on the cheek and shook his brother's hand, he turned to Reanna to see Sam hugging her from behind and whispering in her ear. "When did Sam get so close to Reanna?"

His mom looked up into his eyes. "You are never around to know much lately. They spend a lot of time together when Sam gets out of school. Maybe you should talk to her you might learn some new things."

Shawn nodded at his moms statements and walked over and took the seat next to Reanna. "You seem to have a new best friend?"

"Sam and I have spent a little time getting to know each other, didn't we boo?" Reanna turned to kiss Sam on the cheek.

"She is the bestest step mom a boy could ever have." Sam said as he leaned against Reanna's side. "She plays video games, watches movies and does crossword puzzles with me. I love her dad." His last statement was made as he walked away to go hug his grandmother.

Shawn raised one eyebrow at Sam's last statement and chuckled. "Reanna what are you doing here?"
"I came to see Sam get his certificate then Stan is taking me back home. Just pretend like I am not even here." Reanna waved her hand in his direction.

"I am serious Reanna, I thought we decided you were staying at home to rest." Shawn said sternly.

"Reanna looked at her fingernails and said, "No, you decided I needed to stay home. I decided to come out and play."

"You are risking our child and you make jokes? I do not find this funny." Shawn whispered in her ear.

Reanna leaned over and kissed him, slipping her tongue in his mouth then sat back to observe him. "I love you baby, please let's just enjoy the night."

Shawn gave her a peck on the lips and stressed. "We will talk about this later."

The ceremony began and Shawn and Sam got the community service award presented to them. The program went by quick and Reanna was ready to go home. When Stan escorted her out the door they ran into Melissa. "My you are very pregnant, how are you and Shawn?" Melissa asked in a too sweet voice.

"Shawn and I are fine, we were just about to leave, excuse us Melissa." Reanna went to walk around Melissa.

Melissa reached out and grabbed her arm only to inform her. "That's not what I heard from Shawn. Why don't you ask him what happened the night he stayed at my house when you two got in that argument a month ago."

Reanna felt like she could not breathe and took short, deep breaths. "Get away from me Melissa."

"Maybe you should tell your husband to stay away from me." Melissa winked at her.

Reanna swung her arm and slapped Melissa as hard as she could. Melissa stepped toward her and Stan stepped in between them. "Stop it Melissa you have caused enough pain in this family, just stop!" Melissa turned and stormed away.

Stan turned around and Reanna was near tears, he hugged her and kissed her head. "Trust him Reanna, talk to him."

"I can't breathe, the baby, Stan... "Reanna slurred as she passed out.

Chapter 13

Reanna woke up in the hospital to Stan and Shawn's tense whispering in the far corner of her room.

"Shawn, what are you doing? You give Melissa ammunition to step up to your wife with, are you crazy?"

"It's a long story, I would never hurt Reanna and you know that." Shawn rubbed his hands across his face.

"You could have fooled me; she is in the hospital because of your foolishness. You are going to ruin a good thing. I know you love her but what I don't understand is what is going on with you two." Stan raised his hands in frustration.

Shawn took a deep breathe. "I am so afraid of losing her and the baby that when we disagree I feel it puts stress on the baby. Reanna is so fragile right now, so I work long hours so we won't argue and she can get some rest."

"Shawn, you are going to disagree sometimes, its how you work it out. You ever thought your staying away might stress her out more? She needs you man, she loves you."

Shawn looked over towards Reanna and looked straight into her eyes. He walked over to the bed and took a seat on the edge of the bed. He grabbed her hand and she pulled it out of his grasp and turned her head away from him. "Shawn, I want to be alone." Reanna said on a sob.

Shawn turned her face towards him and looked into her eyes. "Baby, we need to talk and I need to explain some things to you." He turned to Stan. "Stan, could we have some privacy please?" Stan nodded his head and left the room.

As soon as Stan closed the door Reanna laid into Shawn. "Why don't you start by telling me about how you stayed over Melissa's house that night and you did not come home, and then lied to me about it? I trusted you; I am so tired of you and Melissa. I can deal with the Sam situation but I am not going to deal with Melissa and her antics." Reanna sobbed as tears streamed down her face.

"Reanna please calm down and let me explain, you need to stay calm for the baby's sake." Shawn tried to calm her.

"You didn't care about the baby when you were spending time with Melissa. Just go and leave me alone." Reanna continued to cry harder. "Why did you even marry me, didn't you hurt me enough before? I had a good life in Florida and you bring me here for this?"

Shawn sighed and spoke softly. "I married you because I love you, I did sleep over her house that night by mistake, I laid back on the couch to relax and I was so tired from working I fell asleep. I woke up at five in the morning, on the couch, and came straight home. Baby, nothing happened and I did not want to upset you so I did not tell you. I have never cheated on you and I don't intend to start now." Shawn leaned over and wiped her tears off her face.

"I am tired Shawn, so tired." Reanna's voice drifted off as she fell asleep again.

Shawn stood and walked over to the window to look at the view, he was concerned about Reanna and the baby. Life was so easy back in college for them when love was so brand new. He almost went off the deep end when she left last time and knew he could not lose her or the baby now. This was not about him anymore it was about Reanna and the baby he would make sure she was happy and have nothing to worry about. He walked over and kissed her on the cheek and walked out the door. He would definitely make her happy.

Shawn walked into the hospital room the next day to see Sam sitting in Reanna's bed next to her and his mom sitting in the chair next to the bed. Reanna was laughing at something Sam said and when she saw him her laughter stopped. His mom looked over at him and shook her head and Sam smiled at him. "Dad, I was wondering where you were."

Shawn kissed his moms cheek and then responded to Sam. "I was heading over here just to see my favorite little man and my favorite girl."

Sam laughed. "ReRe is your wife; she can't be your favorite girl dad. Even I know that."

Shawn chuckled. "She is my wife and I love her very much. She is also my favorite and only girl." Reanna looked up at Shawn's statement and placed her hands across her stomach as if protecting the baby. Shawn noticed her movement and winced.

"Are you feeling ok Reanna? Shawn asked, genuinely concerned.

"Yes, I am being released later this morning." Reanna looked down at the bed sheets.

His mom stood up and lifted Sam off of the bed. "We have to get you back home young man." Sam walked over and kissed Reanna's hand and waved goodbye to Shawn on his way out the door, closely followed by his grandma.

Shawn stared at her until she looked up at him. "What time are you being released?"

"As soon as you arrived the doctor said I could go. I was waiting until you showed up." Reanna pushed herself up and tried to get out of the bed. "I need to wash off and get dressed, can you help me up?" Shawn walked over and helped her up. Reanna went to the restroom and washed and ended up needing Shawn's help to get dressed.

Shawn helped her and thought she looked beautiful, even pregnant. He was very gentle and kissed her lips when they finished.

She was released within the hour and Shawn brought the BMW around, they drove along in silence for a few miles and Reanna turned to look at Shawn and announced. "I want to go stay with Kandra for awhile."

Shawn's glanced at her and tightened his hands on the steering wheel. He did not answer her and kept driving. "Shawn, I want to go stay with Kandra, I need to get away for awhile. I will be back before the baby is born.

Shawn pulled over to the curb and turned to face her. "Reanna you are six months pregnant and traveling is not good for you right now. I heard the doctor tell you bed rest as soon as you get home. Please don't do this; I won't be able to rest if you go."

Reanna turned away and was quiet, deep in thought, she turned back to Shawn and leaned over and kissed him on the lips. "I need for you to be there for me and spend time with me. I need for you to cut Melissa off completely; she has caused too many problems for us. I need for you to communicate with me about anything and everything, including Sam. I want the closeness we had in college, I just want you back."

Shawn leaned forward and gave her a deep kiss on the lips.

"Done, done and done. I want us back also baby."

Chapter 14

Shawn did a real turnaround, he made sure he came home earlier than usual every night from work and limited his business trips out of town. They spent time watching movies and getting to know each other again. She spent her time in bed resting the last few months of her pregnancy; the doctor had told her that intimacy was ok as long as they were gentle. She was in her eighth month of pregnancy and she was horny as hell. She had a surprise for him tonight when he came home.

Shawn came in from work and took off his clothes, took a shower and put on only flannel night pants while she was watching television. He settled under the covers and she rolled on her side and cuddled next to him with her head on his chest. He tensed and that only made her get bolder, throwing her leg over his thighs. "What are you doing, Reanna?" Shawn asked as he tried to remove her from his side.

"The doctor said it was ok for us to make love again, I miss you." Reanna whined

"I am not going to risk you or the baby by making love to you, it can wait." He sat up to get out of the bed Reanna pushed him down and straddled him, moving fast for an eight month pregnant woman, Shawn thought. She knew he wanted her because she felt his erection against her vagina. She rocked against him and he groaned. She leaned forward and licked his nipples and nibbled on them. He grabbed ahold of her thighs and set the rhythm of the rocking motion. He removed her night shirt saw she wore nothing underneath. Her breasts were heavy with milk and her rounded stomach was sexy as hell.

He rubbed his hands over her breast pinching her nipples lightly, she groaned her pleasure. He rubbed his hands slowly over her rounded stomach knowing his child was growing in there.

"We have to make love with me behind you, spoon fashion." He lowered her to the bed and spooned her from behind. He ran his hands over her breast teasing her nipples until she squirmed for release, he lowered his hand to her moist folds and rubbed her nub. He rubbed her over and over again until he felt her shutter with passion. He propped her leg over his thigh and entered her slowly from behind, she screamed at first contact. He pushed into her until he was all the way inside, then the baby moved. "Our child is protesting the invasion." Shawn said as he rocked against her slowly. Reanna rocked back against him and cried out his name. He reached around and flicked her nub and Reanna came apart in him arms, sobbing as her orgasm hit her. Shawn continued to rock into her until he felt her tighten around him again, he came with her this time crying out her name as his release came.

Epilogue

Eight months later:

Shawn and Reanna stood at the door of their home greeting their guest; this was the wedding reception they put off until after the baby was born. Seven months ago they welcomed Shawn Remington, Jr. into the world. It was a tough fourteen hours of labor but he arrived just as rambunctious as his father.

Reanna looked up at her husband and felt so much love she didn't know what to do. "You ok, baby?" Shawn inquired.

"Yes, just admiring how good my wonderful husband looks." Reanna leaned up and kissed his cheek.

Sam walked over pushing the baby stroller. "I think he wants to spend time with you two." That was usually the line Sam used when he had enough of baby sitting.

"I think he wants to spend more time with his brother." Shawn joked. Sam looked exasperated and dropped his head. Reanna felt sorry for him and excused him to play with his friends.

"Now we are stuck with the baby." Shawn looked exasperated now.

Reanna laughed and picked the baby up out of the stroller, she never felt happier. She kissed Shawn and Shawn, Jr and glanced around at all their friends and family. Her life had come full circle and she knew her life was now complete.........

.

ABOUT THE AUTHOR

I have loved writing and putting my thoughts on paper since I was a child. I finally took the plunge after all these years and published my first e-novel. This has been a dream of mine for years. I love relaxing behind a great romance novel and I want my readers to do the same!!! So to all my readers, enjoy!!!!

I live in Central Florida and work as a supervisor in a prominent restaurant business. I have a Bachelor of Science in Management.

I love to hear from my readers. Please send your feedback to marvayoung@gmail.com

or blog me at:

http://mlyauthorzone.blogspot.com

www.ingramcontent.com/pod-product-compliance
Lightning Source LLC
Chambersburg PA
CBHW070534130626
46555CB00003B/1406